SATURDAY
WITH
LITTLE RABBIT

by *Marjorie Dennis Murray*
illustrations by Stephanie McFetridge Britt

Macmillan Publishing Company   New York
Maxwell Macmillan Canada   Toronto
Maxwell Macmillan International   New York   Oxford   Singapore   Sydney

The text of this book is set in 16 pt. Garamond Light. The illustrations are
rendered in watercolor and pen and ink.

1   3   5   7   9   10   8   6   4   2

Library of Congress Cataloging-in-Publication Data
Murray, Marjorie Dennis. Saturday with Little Rabbit / by Marjorie Dennis Murray ;
illustrations by Stephanie McFetridge Britt. — 1st ed.   p.   cm. Summary: On
Saturday Little Rabbit shares humorous adventures with Woodchuck and Raccoon,
including climbing a tree, building a birdhouse, fishing, and eating strawberry
desserts.
ISBN 0-02-767753-2 [1. Rabbits—Fiction. 2. Animals—Fiction. 3. Friendship—
Fiction.] I. Britt, Stephanie, ill. II. Title. PZ7.M9635Sat 1993
[E]—dc20   91-48362

For Elizabeth, with love,
and for all the children of the Shadyside
Presbyterian Church Nursery School

—*M. D. M.*

To William, and to my family,
for all the love and encouragement;
aloha nui loa

—*S. M. B.*

POND

RACCOON'S
HOUSE

MEADOW

RABBIT'S HOUSE

N
W E
S

CONTENTS

WOODCHUCK'S
HOUSE

PARK

1.
SATURDAY MORNING

Little Rabbit woke up. It was Saturday morning. He hopped out of bed. Little Rabbit put on his jacket. He sat by his window. "I have nothing to do," he said. Across the meadow was Woodchuck's house. I'll go visit Woodchuck, thought Little Rabbit. Maybe Woodchuck has nothing to do.

Little Rabbit went to Woodchuck's house. He knocked on the door. *Knock, knock.* Nobody answered. Woodchuck must have something to do, thought Little Rabbit.

9

In the woods, near the edge of the pond, was Raccoon's house. I'll go visit Raccoon, thought Little Rabbit. Maybe Raccoon has nothing to do.

Little Rabbit went to his friend Raccoon's house. He knocked on the door. *Knock, knock.* Nobody answered. Raccoon must have something to do, thought Little Rabbit. Maybe Raccoon and Woodchuck have something to do together—without me.

Maybe they are picking strawberries together—without me. Maybe they went to the park together—without me. Maybe they went fishing together—without me.

Little Rabbit was very sad. I like to pick strawberries, he thought. I like to go to the park. I like to fish with my friends by the pond.

Little Rabbit went back to his house. There he saw Woodchuck and Raccoon. They were knocking on his door. *Knock, knock.* "Here I am!" cried Little Rabbit.

"Get your bucket," called Raccoon and Woodchuck. "We want to pick strawberries. We came to get you."

Little Rabbit ran to get his bucket. "Wait for me," called Little Rabbit. Then, together, they ran off to the meadow.

2.
AT THE PARK

It was Saturday afternoon. Little Rabbit went to the park with Raccoon.

Raccoon saw a big tree. He climbed to the first branch. "Climb up," said Raccoon to Little Rabbit.

"I don't like to climb trees," said Little Rabbit. "I like to climb on the rocks."

"You're afraid," said Raccoon. "You're afraid to climb trees."

"I'm not afraid," said Little Rabbit.

"There are bugs in trees. There are bugs and spiders and ants. I don't like it when they crawl on me."

"There are no bugs in this tree," said Raccoon. "Climb up."

"No," said Little Rabbit. "There's a spider in that tree."

"That's not a spider," said Raccoon. "It's a leaf." He dropped it on Little Rabbit. Little Rabbit jumped.

"You're afraid," said Raccoon.

"I'm not afraid," said Little Rabbit.

"Then climb on up," said Raccoon.

"No," said Little Rabbit. "There's a snake in that tree."

"That's not a snake," said Raccoon. "It's a stick."

"The stick is moving," said Little Rabbit.

Raccoon jumped down from the tree.

"You were afraid," said Little Rabbit.

"I wasn't afraid," said Raccoon. "I just don't like snakes."

"Even when they're sticks?" asked Little Rabbit, laughing.

"Even when they're sticks," said Raccoon. And Little Rabbit and Raccoon went to climb on the rocks.

3.

THE BIRDHOUSE

Little Rabbit said good-bye to his
friend Raccoon. He went to visit
Woodchuck. Woodchuck was busy in his
yard. "Are you busy?" Little Rabbit asked.

"Yes," said Woodchuck. "I am building
a house."

"It's too small," said Little Rabbit. "You
will not fit in that house."

"It's not for me," said Woodchuck. "It's a birdhouse. Birds like small houses." He cut a hole in the front. He put the roof on the house.

"Can I help?" asked Little Rabbit.

"Do you know how to use a hammer?" asked Woodchuck.

"Sure," said Little Rabbit, "if you hold the nail."

Woodchuck held the nail. Little Rabbit hit it with the hammer.

"Ouch!" cried Woodchuck. "Give me the hammer. I will hit the nails. You hold the roof." Little Rabbit held the roof.

Woodchuck hammered in the nail.

"How will the birds fit through the hole?" asked Little Rabbit. "It's too small."

"This is a bluebird house," said Woodchuck. "The hole is the right size for a bluebird house." He hit a nail with the hammer.

"This house isn't *blue*," said Little Rabbit.

"Of course it's not blue," said Woodchuck. "It's for blue*birds*." He started to hit the nail again.

"What if a redbird moves in?" asked Little Rabbit.

"Ouch!" cried Woodchuck. He put down the hammer. "A redbird is too big for this house. It won't fit through the hole."

"Poor redbird," said Little Rabbit.

"Redbirds don't nest in birdhouses," said Woodchuck. "They nest in trees."

He hammered in the last nail. "Now," said Woodchuck, "we can put it by the birdbath near the meadow."

"Is this the birdbath?" asked Little Rabbit.

"Yes," said Woodchuck.

"It's so big," said Little Rabbit.

"Birds like it big," said Woodchuck.

"Is it just for bluebirds?" asked Little Rabbit.

"It's for all the birds," said Woodchuck. "Bluebirds, redbirds, yellow birds, brown birds…"

"And speckled birds?" asked Little Rabbit.

"And speckled birds," said Woodchuck. "Are you happy now?"

"Yes," said Little Rabbit, and Little Rabbit was happy.

4.

FISHING

The sun was setting. Little Rabbit and Woodchuck went to Raccoon's house to go fishing.

The three friends sat by the pond together. A fish jumped out of the water. "You can't catch me!" cried the fish.

"I don't want to catch you," said Little Rabbit. "I just want to sit by the pond."

"I will catch you," said Raccoon. "I am hungry for fish dinner."

The fish jumped out of the water. "You can't catch me!" he cried.

Raccoon said to Woodchuck, "Help me catch the fish and we will have fish dinner."

Woodchuck cast out his fishing line. Raccoon held out his net. Little Rabbit sat by the pond.

The fish leaped out of the water. He
jumped over the net. "You can't catch
me!" he cried. He swam to the middle of
the pond.

Woodchuck dropped his fishing line. Raccoon dropped his net. They jumped into their boat. They rowed out on the water. Little Rabbit sat by the pond.

The fish leaped out of the water. He jumped over the boat. "You can't catch me!" he cried.

Woodchuck and Raccoon chased him in their boat. They rowed around the pond.

The fish swam close to Little Rabbit.
He jumped into Little Rabbit's lap. "You
can't catch me!" he cried.

"Hold on to that fish!" called
Raccoon and Woodchuck.

The fish leaped out of Little Rabbit's lap. He missed the water. He landed in the weeds. He couldn't swim away.

"Help me, Little Rabbit!" cried the fish.

Little Rabbit picked up the fish. He put it back in the water. Woodchuck and Raccoon rowed to shore. "Where's our fish dinner?" they asked.

"In the pond," said Little Rabbit, "where that silly fish belongs."

5.

STRAWBERRY PIE

It was Saturday evening. Little Rabbit baked a strawberry pie. He took it to Raccoon's house. He knocked on the door.

"Come in," said Raccoon. A bucket of strawberries was on the table. Raccoon opened his oven. He had baked strawberry muffins. So Raccoon had some pie and Little Rabbit had a muffin.

"Maybe Woodchuck would like some pie," said Little Rabbit. "Maybe Woodchuck would like a muffin."

The two friends went to Woodchuck's
house. They knocked on the door.

"Come in," said Woodchuck. A bucket
of strawberries was on the floor.
Woodchuck opened his oven. He had
baked strawberry cake.

Little Rabbit took strawberries out
of the bucket. He put them on top of
the cake.

Then they sat down to eat. Little Rabbit
had some pie. Woodchuck had some
cake. And Raccoon had a muffin. Then
Raccoon had some cake. Woodchuck had
some pie. And Little Rabbit had a muffin.
Woodchuck pushed away his plate.

"I cannot eat another strawberry," said Woodchuck.

"I cannot look at another strawberry," said Raccoon.

"I can't even *think* about strawberries," Little Rabbit said.

So the three friends took the cake, muffins, and pie outside.

Bluebirds were in the birdhouse. Redbirds were in the tree. A flock of speckled birds was on the roof.

"Here are strawberry muffins for you," said Raccoon to the redbirds.

"Here is strawberry cake for you," Woodchuck said to the bluebirds.

"We have strawberry pie for you," said Little Rabbit to the speckled birds on the roof.

It was getting late. Little Rabbit said
good-bye to his friends. "I'll see you
tomorrow," he said.

Little Rabbit went home. He took off
his jacket. He hopped into bed.

Little Rabbit looked out his window at
the stars. He saw fishes and birds and
hammers and buckets.

Soon his eyes began to close. "Good-
night, Saturday," said Little Rabbit.
He wanted to say, "I'll see you
next week," but Little Rabbit fell
fast asleep.

47